Greetings.
I am Princess Allura
of planet Altea.
Ten thousand years ago
Planet Altea was once ruled
by my father, King Alfor.

He built five spaceships.
Each ship looked like a lion.
The lions were flown
by pilots called Paladins.
When the spaceships joined
together, they formed
a super-robot called Voltron.

DreamWorks VOLTRON
LEGENDARY DEFENDER

Allura's Story

By Cala Spinner

Illustrated by Patrick Spaziante

Ready-to-Read

Simon Spotlight
New York   London   Toronto   Sydney   New Delhi

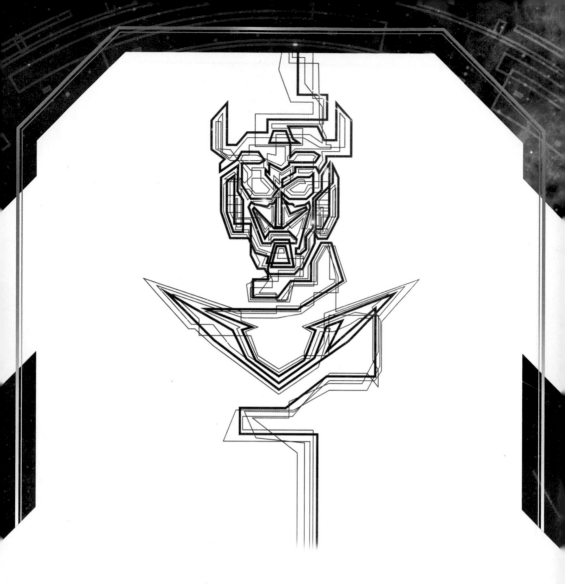

SIMON SPOTLIGHT
An imprint of Simon & Schuster Children's Publishing Division
1230 Avenue of the Americas, New York, New York 10020
This Simon Spotlight edition December 2018
For information about
special discounts for bulk purchases, please contact Simon & Schuster Special Sales at
1-866-506-1949 or business@simonandschuster.com.
Manufactured in the United States of America 1118 LAK
2 4 6 8 10 9 7 5 3 1
ISBN 978-1-5344-3035-8 (hc)
ISBN 978-1-5344-3034-1 (pbk)
ISBN 978-1-5344-3036-5 (eBook)

My father and four other pilots
were the first Paladins.
They became good friends.

One pilot was named Zarkon.
He was an emperor who ruled
the Galra people.

Zarkon was my father's best friend.
He was very kind to my family.
He gave me a gift
when I was a child.
It was a helmet.

As a young girl,
I dreamed of becoming
a Paladin of Voltron.

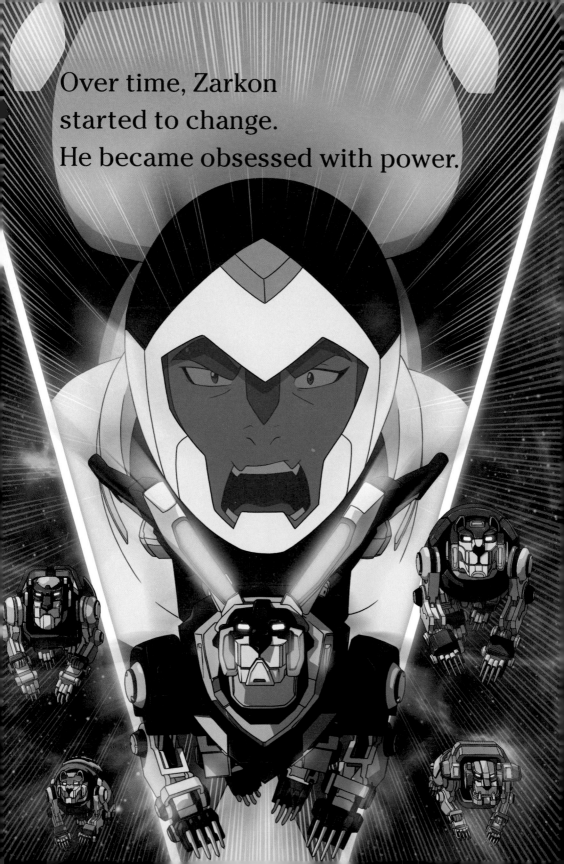

Over time, Zarkon
started to change.
He became obsessed with power.

He wanted to control everyone
and everything in the galaxy.
He turned on the other Paladins.
He even attacked Altea!

I wanted to stop Zarkon.
I wanted to form Voltron and
fight Zarkon's army—the Galra.
I tried to convince my father
and Coran, his advisor.

But my father did not agree.
He did not think we could win.
He had another plan.

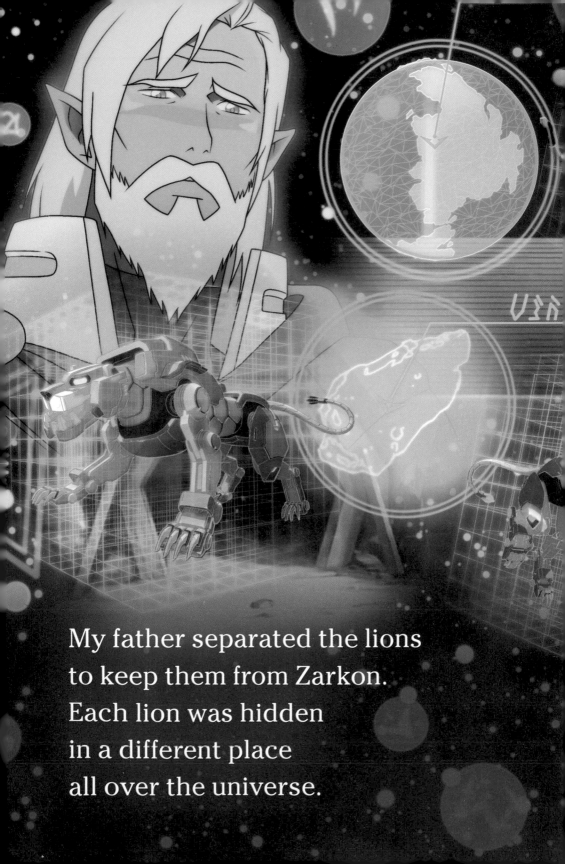

My father separated the lions
to keep them from Zarkon.
Each lion was hidden
in a different place
all over the universe.

He hoped that one day
Voltron would be able to
stop Zarkon once and for all.

Then my father put me
in a cryo-pod.
There were four Altean mice
with me.

Coran was placed in
a cryo-pod too.
He would be *my* advisor now.
We slept in the pods
for ten thousand years.

Coran and I woke up
to a very different universe.
Everything we knew,
including Altea, was gone.
Five people from Planet Earth
stood before us.

At first, I was confused.
Who were these people?
Why were their ears so . . . odd?
Then I realized what
had happened.

The Paladins of old were gone.
My father was gone.
I knew that I had to
carry out his plans.
It was time to form Voltron again.
I sensed the lions' locations.

We found them.
Then each of the five Earthlings
formed a bond with the lions.
They became
the new Paladins of Voltron.
Then we worked together to stop
one of Zarkon's ships.

Still, it was not easy.
The new Paladins did not
always get along.
I didn't know what to do.
I thought of my father
and his leadership.

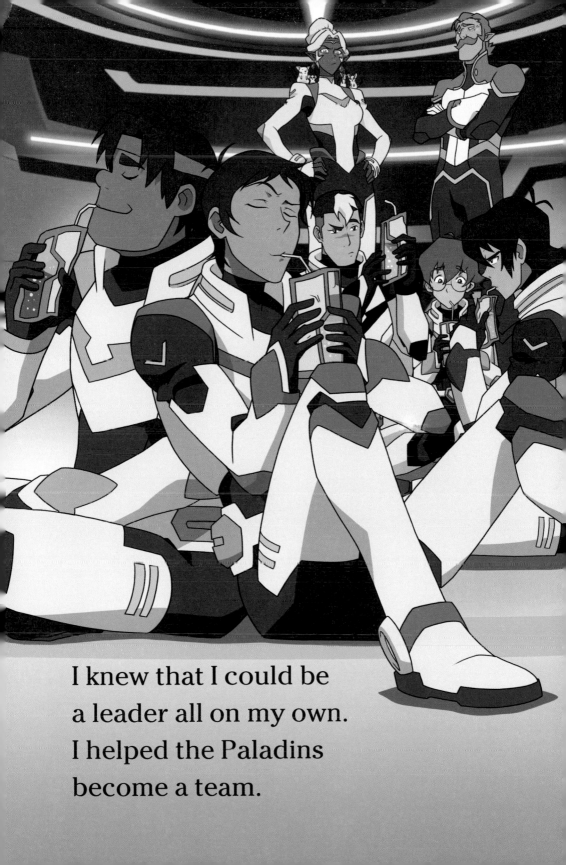

I knew that I could be
a leader all on my own.
I helped the Paladins
become a team.

Together, we freed planets that had been under Zarkon's rule— like the Balmerans. Zarkon made them work underground in their planet's crystal mines.

I also had to be brave.
I learned how to use my powers
to save people.

Taking on the Galra
was not easy.
Sometimes we failed.
After one battle,
we became one
pilot short.

The Blue Lion needed a new pilot.
Without all the lions,
we couldn't form Voltron.
Voltron is important to me
because I believe
in freedom and peace.

I walked over to the Blue Lion.
I tried talking nicely to it,
but it did not wake up.

I told the lion about my father.
Then I told the lion
that I wanted peace.
The lion listened.
Then it chose me as its Paladin.
My dream came true!

As an Altean,
I have many powers,
such as superstrength.

I also have a whip.
Coran says I need
to be careful.
But it is fun to swing!

I started life as a princess,
and now I am a Paladin.
One day I will restore peace and
freedom to the universe.
I hope that I make
my father proud.